# The Abandoned Kitten

The Royal Society for the Prevention of Cruelty to Animals is the UK's largest animal charity. They rescue, look after and rehome hundreds of thousands of animals each year in England and Wales. They also offer advice on caring for all animals and campaign to change laws that will protect them. Their work relies on your support, and buying this book helps them save animals' lives.

www.rspca.org.uk

# The Abandoned Kitten

By Sue Mongredien

Illustrated by Jon Davis

SCHOLASTIC

First published in the UK in 2013 by Scholastic Children's Books
An imprint of Scholastic Ltd
Euston House, 24 Eversholt Street
London, NW1 1DB, UK
Registered office: Westfield Road, Southam, Warwickshire, CV47 0RA
SCHOLASTIC and associated logos are trademarks
and/or registered trademarks of Scholastic Inc.

Text copyright © RSPCA, 2013
Illustration copyright © RSPCA, 2013

ISBN 978 1407 13324 9

RSPCA name and logo are trademarks of RSPCA used by
Scholastic Ltd under licence from RSPCA Trading Ltd.
Scholastic will donate a minimum amount to the RSPCA from
every book sold. Such amount shall be paid to RSPCA Trading Limited,
which pays all its taxable profits to the RSPCA. Registered in
England and Wales Charity No. 219099
www.rspca.org.uk

A CIP catalogue record for this book is available
from the British Library.

Printed and bound by CPI Group (UK) Ltd, Croydon, CR0 4YY
Papers used by Scholastic Children's Books are made
from wood grown in sustainable forests.

9 10

www.scholastic.co.uk

It was a wild, windy day and nine-year-old Lily Hart was playing football in the garden with her family. Dad was in goal, while Mum, Lily and her twin brothers, Max and Jacob, tried to score against him. Meg the dog was playing, too, of course, barking with excitement, her tail wagging non-stop.

The ball came to Lily, who kicked it up the garden towards the goal. Dad dived in an attempt to catch it but slid on the mud and slipped over. The ball flew straight past him and into the back of the net.

"And she SCOOOOORES!" Lily cheered, racing around the garden, her arms out wide. She high-fived Max, Jacob and Mum, and then Meg bounced over as if she wanted to join in the celebrations as well.

"Hey, Megster," Lily said, crouching down and patting her. Meg was an energetic collie cross who liked nothing better than being outside with her family – especially if there was a ball involved. "Did you see that goal? Put it there!"

Meg woofed as if she could understand every word, and sat on her hind legs so that she could give Lily a paw. "Good girl," Lily said, shaking it gently with a grin.

Dad picked himself up, his calves covered in mud. It had rained heavily the night before as well as that morning, and the garden was very boggy. "Well done, Lils," he said, grabbing the ball. "Tell you what, guys, the next person to score is the champion. I need a cup of tea."

"Sounds good to me," Mum agreed.

"I'm definitely going to be the champion," Jacob said at once.

"No way," Max argued. "It's so going to be me."

Lily smiled to herself. Her brothers were six years old and *very* competitive. They were also identical, with the same sandy-brown tufty hair, blue eyes and upturned noses. Jacob had a few more freckles than Max, and Max had a mole at the side of his chin, but unless you knew them well, it was hard to tell them apart.

Dad raised an eyebrow. "Well, there's

only one way to find out," he said. "Ready? Here we go."

Dad kicked the ball and it flew through the air. Jacob, Max and Lily jostled one another as they rushed towards the spot where they thought it would land. But one member of the family beat them all to it. Meg leaped high off the ground to head the ball down, then chased it back across the garden as it rolled towards the goal. By sheer luck, the ball bounced right through Dad's legs and into the net!

Everyone roared with laughter. "Meg's the champion!" Lily cried, running to make a fuss of her. "What a clever dog."

Meg's tail thumped against Lily's legs and she woofed happily. She'd been a member of the Hart family almost as long as Lily. Mum worked part-time at the nearby RSPCA centre as an Animal Care

Assistant, looking after all the animals who came in needing treatment and helping find them new homes. Meg had been brought there as a tiny puppy back when Lily was just a few months old.

Meg had been separated from her mother and was still too young to feed herself, so she needed to be hand-fed with bottles of special milk before she could be weaned on to puppy food. Mum was in charge of looking after Meg, and brought her home so that she could care for her around the clock. It wasn't long before Mum and Dad both adored Meg, and decided to keep her as their family pet.

Lily was too young to remember Meg arriving, but there were lots of photos in the family album showing them sharing Mum's lap, or curled up asleep next to each other on a blanket. Then, as Meg grew stronger and Lily started crawling, they'd got into all sorts of mischief together, happily emptying kitchen cupboards when Mum's back was turned or pulling baubles off the tree at Christmas time.

"Well done, Meg," said Mum, coming over to pat her. "A worthy champion indeed."

"Quick, get on the phone to Manchester United," Dad joked, scooping up the ball. "They'll sign up a super-striker like Meg in a shot."

"They could pay her in dog biscuits," suggested Jacob, and Meg woofed again, her ears pricking up at the word "biscuits".

"She could wear a red shirt with her name on the back," said Max, laughing. "And special little football boots!"

Lily giggled at the thought. "Don't worry, Meg," she said. "We wouldn't let them have you anyway, even if they offered us millions of pounds. You're *our* dog, aren't you?"

Lily's last words were drowned out by a loud rumble of thunder overhead. A cold gust of wind snaked around the garden, shaking the branches of the plum tree and flattening the grass. Lily shivered and rubbed her bare arms as she looked up at the sky. Dark clouds had appeared, blotting out the sun.

"You're *all* champions," Mum said, "but we'd better get inside, quick. Looks like it's about to start pouring. Run!"

Once they'd raced back indoors, everyone peeled off their muddy things and put on clean clothes. Dad made a jug of orange squash for the children and produced a packet of biscuits while Meg drank splashily from her bowl of water. Within moments, the rain was pattering down again.

Lily leaned against the warm radiator, glad to be indoors out of the cold and wet. "That's the end of our game of football," she said, staring through the window.

"Not necessarily," said Mum. "How about we play blow football instead?"

"What's that?" Jacob asked, as Mum pulled a handful of straws from the kitchen drawer.

Mum grinned. "A perfect rainy-day game," she replied mysteriously. "Boys, did I see a ping-pong ball up in your bedroom? Could you go and fetch it, please?"

Dad cleared the kitchen table and

Mum put empty shoeboxes at either end, their open sides facing the middle. Jacob and Max rushed back in, Max triumphantly clutching the white ping-pong ball, and Mum set it carefully in the centre of the table.

"Right," she said. "We'll play kids versus grown-ups. Everyone blows through a straw, trying to send the ball into the opposite team's goal – the shoeboxes. You need to keep your hands behind your backs because touching the ball is not allowed. OK?"

Lily laughed. Her family were a bit crazy! She knew that her best friend Martha's parents wouldn't dream of puffing a ping-pong ball around their kitchen table until they were pink in the cheeks. But the game turned out to be great fun, with everyone blowing through

their straws like mad whenever the ball rolled their way.

Meg seemed a bit confused by all the giggling and cheering but she was very helpful whenever the ball rolled off the table, rushing to fetch it as it bounced around the kitchen floor. She'd bring it back each time, dropping it gently into Mum's hand and wagging her tail.

The score was Kids: 5, Grown-ups: 3 when the phone rang and interrupted the game. Dad put down his straw and went to answer the call. "Hello? . . . Yes," his voice came from the living room. "Sure, I'll just get her."

"It's for you," Dad said to Mum as he came back into the kitchen. "Nicky from work."

Mum hurried out of the room at once. "Hi, Nicky," Lily heard her say. "Oh goodness! When? Poor little things. Yes, of course I will. No problem. I'll be right there."

Lily couldn't help wondering who the "poor little things" were and what had happened. All sorts of ill and injured animals came into the RSPCA centre every day; some had been in accidents or hadn't been well treated. Sometimes, if the animals needed urgent care, extra staff would be called in to help on their days off. Because the Hart family lived so close to the centre, Mum never minded pitching in if there was an emergency. Lily felt proud of Mum for what she did. *It must be the best job in the world, making scared, hurt animals feel better*, she thought.

Mum reappeared in the kitchen a few minutes later wearing her jacket and shoes. "I've got to pop into work," she told them. "Something's come up."

"What is it?" Lily asked. "Is it serious?"

"I'd better dash. I'll tell you when I get back," Mum said, sounding distracted. "See you all later, OK?"

Lily watched her hurry away, wondering what might be happening at the centre that was so urgent. Meg whined as the front door closed behind Mum, and Lily bent down to give her a hug. "Don't worry," she told her dog. "She'll be home soon."

# 2

With Mum out, and the boys supposedly tidying their messy bedroom, Lily decided to get on with her homework. She had some maths puzzles to work out and a list of spellings to learn for a test. It was hard to concentrate, though, when she kept thinking about the animals Mum might be looking after at the RSPCA centre. She hoped everything was OK.

"Have you heard from Mum yet?" she asked Dad when he came into the kitchen a bit later.

Dad shook his head. "Not a sausage,"

he said. "How's the homework going? Do you need any help?"

Lily closed her exercise book. "I'll do it later," she said, wrinkling her nose.

Dad gave her a thoughtful look, as if he knew her mind was elsewhere. "Tell you what," he said, "why don't we make a nice cake for tea? Mum deserves a treat for working so hard."

Lily smiled. "Good idea," she said.

Once they'd washed their hands, Lily helped weigh out the butter and sugar, and tipped them into a big mixing bowl. "It won't be long until I need to make a special cake for you," Dad said, getting eggs out of the fridge, "what with your birthday next month. Have you thought about what kind of cake you might like this year?"

"Chocolate, please," Lily said at once. Dad was a really good baker, and made the most amazing cakes for everyone. Last year, he'd baked her a cake in the shape of a dog's head, complete with a pink iced tongue hanging out of its smiling mouth. "But that's still ages away."

"Ahh, you wait, the weeks will fly by," Dad said, passing Lily a wooden spoon. "Right – let's get mixing."

Lily enjoyed helping Dad in the kitchen. He was an artist, illustrating storybooks and greetings cards for a living, and he saw cookery as another chance to be creative. Some of his cake decorations turned out almost as beautiful as his paintings and drawings!

Lily's favourite picture by Dad was one that hung above the mantelpiece in the living room. In the painting, the Harts were riding on the back of a smiling green dragon, looking as if they were flying off to have a wonderful adventure

together. Even Meg was included in the painting, sitting on the dragon's back with Lily's arms around her. It made Lily smile every time she looked at it.

"Hmm," Dad said as Lily sifted the flour into the bowl. "What can we put in this cake to give it some extra zing?"

"Lemon juice?" Lily suggested.

"Good thinking," he replied. "And how about a handful of chocolate chips and some grated orange zest, too?"

"Yum," Lily said approvingly. "Mum's going to love it."

The cake smelled delicious as it baked, and Lily helped Dad with the washing up. She began to feel hungry and glanced up at the clock to see when it would be teatime. To her surprise, it was almost five o'clock already. Mum had been gone for hours now! She and the rest of the

RSPCA team must be really busy. When was she going to come home?

Once the cake had cooled, Lily and Dad covered it in white glossy icing, then decorated it with candied orange and lemon slices around the edge. Then Dad's phone buzzed.

"Aha!" he said, reading a text. "That's your mum. She'll be home in about fifteen minutes." He peered in the fridge. "How does pizza for tea sound?"

Lily grinned. "Sounds perfect."

A short while later, Meg barked and they heard the key turn in the front door. "Mum's home!" Max cried.

"Brilliant timing," Dad said, switching off the oven and putting a handful of cutlery on the table.

"We're in the kitchen!" Lily called.

Mum appeared holding an animal carrier. "Hi, everyone," she said, setting it carefully on the table. Then she sniffed. "Mmm, something smells nice in here."

"Hi, Mum," Lily said. "Is everything all right? What's in there?"

Dad went over to kiss Mum and looked into the cat carrier. His eyes widened as he saw what she'd brought in. "Oh my goodness," he said. "What have we here?"

"Three little babies who need some extra looking after," Mum replied, then smiled at Lily and the boys. "Come over and have a peep – but be really quiet, won't you? I don't want them to be scared."

Lily was bursting with curiosity as she, Jacob and Max went over to see. Mum carefully opened the carrier and Lily

gasped with excitement as she saw three
bundles of fluff inside, curled up on a
soft blue blanket, with a hot-water bottle
keeping them warm. They were the
tiniest kittens she'd ever seen!

"Oh, Mum," she whispered, resisting
the urge to reach in and stroke them. She
knew that they might be very poorly, and
that she needed to check before touching
them. "They're so small. Are they OK?"

Mum gave her a smile. "I'm going to do my best to look after them," she said, which didn't really answer Lily's question.

"What *are* they?" Max asked, peering in. "Are they hamsters?"

"They're kittens!" Lily replied.

"We think they're only a week old," Mum added, "which is why their eyes haven't opened yet. They're pretty helpless right now."

"They don't look like proper kittens," Jacob said, hanging back doubtfully.

Mum smiled. "They're just babies," she said. "And they don't have a mummy to look after them, so I'm going to have to be their mummy for a short while, and take care of them here. Just like a real cat mummy, I'll be taking them everywhere with me. So when I'm at home they'll be here, and when I go to work they'll come with me as well!"

Meg seemed curious about the new arrivals. She kept walking back and forth, and sniffing the air around the table. Then she made a funny whining sound.

"Good girl. It's all right," Mum told her, reaching down and stroking her silky head. "You're still top dog in this house, don't worry."

Lily gazed in at the kittens. One was black all over, another was black with white paws and a white mark on its face, and the third and smallest kitten was a tabby, with grey and black markings. They were very sweet with their crumpled-looking ears and tightly shut eyes, but Jacob was right: they didn't look like other kittens she'd seen. She'd always thought of kittens as being full of energy, tumbling over each other

and playing with everything in sight. These three, by contrast, seemed hardly able to move. No wonder Mum had called them "poor little things" on the phone!

Just then, the black kitten opened its mouth and gave a teeny-tiny mew, and Lily's heart melted at the sound.

"I think somebody's hungry again," Mum said. "Let's give kitty a feed."

"Can I help?" Lily asked.

"Of course," Mum said. "Without their mummy around, we need to feed them with special kitten milk. I've brought some home with me."

"What happened to their mum?" Lily asked, watching as Mum popped the lid off a large tin full of creamy-white powder. "Is she still at the centre?"

Mum shook her head. "We don't know where she is, unfortunately," she replied, tipping a scoop of powder into a jug and measuring out boiled water from the kettle. "All we know is that these three were found at the end of a garden in the next village – soaking wet and shivering. The mother cat was nowhere to be seen."

"Poor babies," Lily said, feeling sad. She hated to think of them lying there, cold and wet, without their mum to take care of them.

"The lady who brought them into the centre said it was only by chance that she found them at all," Mum went on. "She was just nipping out to the shop when she spotted them under the hedge in her front garden. She got them to us in the nick of time."

Jacob looked upset. "Why did their mummy leave them there?" he asked.

"Maybe she didn't have a choice," Mum replied, whisking the powder into the water until it looked like smooth, creamy milk. "There," she said. "This substitute milk has all the goodness they need to help them grow properly but isn't too rich for their little tummies. Kittens don't drink the milk we drink."

More squeaks were coming from the cat carrier now, and Lily peered in to see all three kittens mewing pitifully.

"Nearly ready, guys," she said softly.
"Milk's on its way."

"Why don't you wash your hands and stroke them very gently?" Mum suggested to Lily, filling a dropper with the milk. "That might comfort them until I can feed them all."

Lily quickly washed her hands and stroked the tiny kittens with her finger. Their bodies were soft and warm. "It's all right," she whispered. "Don't worry. We know you're hungry."

"I'm hungry, too," Max said at that moment, suddenly remembering the pizzas. "Are *we* allowed something to eat?"

"Definitely," said Dad. "Wash your hands and then sit at the table, boys. Pizza number one is about to be served and pizza number two can wait until the kitten feeding is over."

"I can wait till later," Lily said at once. "Shall I carry on helping you, Mum?"

"Yes, please," Mum replied. "If you could keep comforting the other two while I feed the first one, that would be wonderful."

Everyone watched Mum as she scooped the black-and-white kitten out of the cat carrier. It was so small it easily fitted into her hand – just a handful of fluff with a tiny scrap of a tail. Lily glanced up at the window and saw that the rain was still pouring down outside. She was so glad the kittens had been found.

Meg came over to smell the kitten, but Dad gently pulled her away by her collar. "Let's look from a distance, Meg," he said, patting her side. "Good girl."

Mum sat down with the kitten cuddled on her lap and then, using a small dropper, she carefully squeezed a few drops of warm milk into the kitten's open pink mouth.

The kitten spluttered a little before swallowing the milk. Then it opened its mouth again for more.

Lily watched, still gently stroking the other two. "Is that one a boy or a girl kitten, Mum?" she asked.

"This is one of the boys," Mum replied. "There are two boys and a girl."

"Two boys and a girl, eh?" Dad said, putting plates of pizza slices on the table for Jacob and Max. "Now where have I heard that before?"

"The brothers are the coolest," Max said immediately, nudging Jacob.

Jacob nodded, his mouth full. "The brothers are the best," he agreed.

Lily caught Mum's eye and they both smiled. "Which is the girl?" Lily asked.

"The little tabby," Mum said. "She's the smallest of the bunch, which probably means she's the youngest."

Lily stroked the tabby, who had pretty stripy markings. "You're definitely the cutest," she whispered to her. "Don't listen to my brothers, OK?"

"There," said Mum after a few minutes, when the black-and-white kitten had drunk enough. "One down, two to feed."

"That was quick," Dad commented, forking some salad into his mouth.

"Their tummies are so small it doesn't take long to fill them up," Mum replied. "Although it does mean that they'll be hungry again in a few hours." She gently returned the black-and-white kitten to the blanket and took out the all-black kitten, who was squeaking sorrowfully. "Your turn now, little one," she said soothingly.

"So the kittens will need feeding again when we're in bed?" Lily asked. "And in the middle of the night?"

"Yes," said Mum. "Every two and a half

hours or thereabouts. Just like you three when you were tiny babies."

"Cool," said Max. "Can we stay up all night, too?"

"No chance." Dad said, laughing. "Finish that pizza, then you can have some cake."

Lily had been so excited by the kittens, she'd forgotten all about the cake. "Oh yes!" she said. "Me and Dad baked it especially for you, Mum."

"Wow," Mum said, looking pleased. "Kind children, a pizza-baking husband and a cake . . . what a lucky mum I am."

*Woof!* went Meg. "Not forgetting the best dog ever," Mum said, with a smile.

# 3

Now that he had been fed, the first kitten's tummy was round and full like a little drum, and he dozed contentedly. "Let's feed your brother next," Mum said, cradling the all-black kitten. She glanced in at the tabby. "Little sister might need some extra help."

"What do you mean?" Lily asked.

"Well, she had difficulty drinking back at the centre," Mum explained. "I thought I'd feed the boys quickly, and then I can spend a bit longer with her."

While the second kitten drank his milk,

Lily continued to stroke the tabby, whose squeaks had grown fainter, almost as if she was too hungry to meow. "Your turn next," Lily assured her. "Not long to wait."

Meg was still watching everything with great interest, and Dad patted her fondly. "This reminds me of when our Meg was tiny," he said. "It doesn't seem five minutes since Mum was sitting there feeding *her* with a bottle."

"I was just thinking the same thing," Mum said, then smiled at the children. "It's hard to believe it now she's such a lovely bouncy dog, but Meg was left all alone, too, a tiny, hungry puppy." She glanced at Meg, who was gazing adoringly back. "So tiny she could fit in my pocket, can you believe?"

"You'd need massive pockets to fit Meg

in one now," Jacob said, his eyes wide. "Pockets like sleeping bags!"

"You've never heard such sad little whimpers as when we first got Meg," Dad said. "I thought it was you crying, Lily, until I saw our new arrival. Baby number two, so weak and small. Poor girly." He patted her again and she wagged her tail happily. "You turned out all right, though, hey?" he said.

The boys finished their cake, and Dad went upstairs to help them with their bath. Then there was just the tabby kitten left to feed. She had stopped mewing altogether now, and lay still and quiet, as if her last scrap of energy had gone.

"Come on, poppet," Mum said, gently lifting her out and laying her on her lap.

Lily watched closely. The tabby seemed very limp and was barely moving. "Is she all right?" she asked, feeling alarmed.

"She's gone through a bit of an ordeal," Mum said, positioning the dropper at the tabby's mouth. "Come on, lovely. Open your mouth for me."

The tabby still didn't move as Mum tried to tempt her with the milk. "Here we are," Mum coaxed. "Nice warm milk.

Let's see if you can manage to drink something this time."

Lily bit her lip. Why wasn't the tabby kitten responding? Something didn't feel right. "Did she have any milk earlier at the RSPCA centre?" she asked.

"Not much," Mum said, gently prising open the tabby's mouth. "Come on, little one. You really need to drink this." She slid the end of the dropper inside and carefully squeezed a drop of milk into the kitten's mouth.

Lily held her breath. Nothing happened for a long, awful moment, and Lily was just starting to fear the worst when the kitten stirred feebly and coughed.

Mum looked concerned but tried again, giving the dropper another tiny squeeze so that a single creamy drop of milk fell into the kitten's mouth. Once again the tabby merely coughed and spluttered, and the milk dribbled straight out on to Mum's jeans.

"Oh dear." Mum sighed. "This one still can't suck the milk like her brothers."

"But she'll learn, right?" Lily asked. Her tummy felt funny as she gazed from the helpless kitten up to Mum's anxious face.

Mum didn't reply for a moment. "I hope so, love," she said, trying once more to feed the tabby. "But. . ."

"But what?" Lily asked. She was starting to feel really frightened for the kitten.

"Well, these kittens are very young to be without their mother," Mum replied eventually. "We've got to be prepared for the fact that they might not survive, unfortunately. All three of them are very weak, and I'm afraid that being out in the cold rain might have made them ill." She gazed down at the tabby, who was still spluttering over the milk. "I hate to say it, but this little baby may not even make it through the night."

Tears swelled in Lily's eyes. "You mean she could die?"

Mum reached out and put a hand on Lily's. "Hopefully not," she said. "I'm going to do my very best to keep these kittens warm and fed, but I can't say that everything will be all right just yet. The next few days are critical." She glanced up at the ceiling, through which they could hear the noisy rumpus of Jacob and Max having their bath. "Perhaps it's best not to tell your brothers about this, OK?" she added. "They're too young to understand."

Lily nodded, feeling hopeless. She couldn't bear the thought of any of the kittens not surviving. Then she felt a

surge of determination. She crouched
beside Mum and stroked the tiny tabby.
"Come on," she urged. "Let's have some
girl power, hey? Drink your milk. It'll
make you feel much better. For me?"

Lily and Mum spent the next few
minutes trying to feed the kitten, both
coaxing and encouraging her in soft
voices. At last, Mum got a couple of

drops of milk inside her, and then the kitten seemed to doze off again. "It's hard to tell if she's asleep when her eyes are shut the whole time," Mum said, "but she's had a bit to drink, at least. I think that's all we can do for now."

"Do you think it's enough?" Lily asked, feeling tense.

"Let's hope so," Mum said, carefully lifting the tabby back on to the blanket with her brothers. "Now there's one more important job to do before their next meal."

Mum explained that usually after feeding, the mother cat would wash the kittens, licking them with her rough tongue. This sensation helped the kittens digest the milk properly and go to the toilet. She laughed. "Don't worry, I'm not going to lick the kittens myself," she said, seeing Lily's expression. "I'll use some damp cotton wool instead. It'll work just as well."

Despite her worries, Lily found herself giggling at the thought of Mum licking the kittens. "Phew," she said. "Can I watch?"

"Of course you can," Mum said.

Mum gently wiped the kittens, then found an empty, clean cardboard box from the utility room. "I'll make a bed for them in here," she said, putting it on the table. Next she boiled the kettle and topped up the kittens' hot-water bottle, then placed it with their blanket into the box. Last of all, she scooped up the kittens, one by one, and put them into their cosy new home.

"OK, guys, sleep well," she said to them. "More milk in a few hours." She put an arm around Lily. "Now it's our turn to eat. You must be starving."

While Mum washed her hands and took their pizza out of the bottom oven, Lily stayed with the kittens, reaching in and stroking them all very gently. She could feel their tiny ribs rising and falling as they breathed. "I'm sorry you don't have a mummy," she whispered to them. "It must have been really scary, being on your own out in the rain. But you're safe with us now, and we're going to look after you the best we can, OK?"

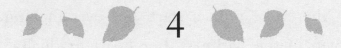 4

The kittens were still snoozing in the
box when Lily went up to bed that
night, but she found it hard to get to
sleep herself for worrying about them.
*Please let them be all right*, she kept
thinking. *Please let them still be here in
the morning.*

When at last she managed to drift off,
Lily fell into a series of dreams about
the kittens. She dreamed that she went
down for breakfast and the kitchen was
full of kittens – black ones, ginger ones,
grey ones, tortoiseshell ones – all over

the table, climbing the curtains, and even riding on Meg's back.

She woke with a start, her eyes flicking open in the darkness, her heart gradually slowing. It was just a silly dream, she told herself, but then she immediately wondered how the real kittens were getting on. Rolling over, she saw that it was half past one in the morning. She hoped the tiny tabby had managed to feed better so far during the night.

A moment later, she heard Mum and Dad's bedroom door open with a creak, then soft footsteps outside her room. She listened as the footsteps went padding down the stairs and realized it must be Mum getting up to give the kittens another feed. That only made Lily feel more wide awake than ever – there was no way she could fall back asleep without

knowing what was happening in the
kitchen. Were the kittens all right?

Lily couldn't stay in bed another
minute. She got up and pulled on her
dressing gown before tiptoeing downstairs
after Mum.

Rain was still speckling the windows
but the kitchen was bright and cosy as
Lily crept in. Meg was curled up in her
basket and opened one eye to see her,
greeting her with a soft woof.

Mum was mixing up another feed for the kittens but turned round at the sound. "Lily!" she said in surprise. "What are you doing up at this time of night? Can't you sleep?"

Lily didn't answer. She barely heard what Mum was saying. "Are they OK?" she asked anxiously, walking over to the cardboard box. She could hear the high-pitched hungry squeaks the kittens were making and gazed in, rapidly counting one, two, three animals. She let out a breath of relief and reached in to stroke them. "Hello," she said softly. "Is it milk time again?"

"It certainly is," said Mum, filling a dropper with the warm kitten milk. "The two black ones have been guzzling it down since you went up to bed. They seem to be sucking better already, which is really good news."

"How about the little tabby?" Lily asked, running a finger gently down her soft back. "Has she started feeding properly as well?"

Mum hesitated. "Not yet," she said after a moment, tightening the lid of the dropper. "But I'll keep on trying. Hopefully this time she'll take a bit more."

"Can I try feeding her?" Lily asked.

"Not tonight, love," Mum said. "I've got to do this really carefully, so that exactly the right amount of milk goes into her mouth. But why don't you take one of the boys? They've got the hang of it, so they're easier to feed. Have this dropper, and I'll use a different one."

Lily sat down, and Mum placed the black kitten in the crook of her right arm.

He felt warm and wriggly as he nestled
into her sleeve. He knew exactly what
to do and opened his little pink mouth
expectantly for the milk. Lily smiled.
"He's like a baby bird," she said, carefully
positioning the end of the dropper in
his mouth and giving the rubbery top a

gentle squeeze. "Good boy," she whispered happily, hearing him swallow the milk in the next moment. "Clever boy, that's it."

Meanwhile, Mum had sat down with the tabby. She was mewing weakly but still didn't seem to know what to do when the milk squirted into her mouth, either spluttering or letting it dribble down her chin.

"Come on, girly," Mum coaxed. "Don't spit it out. We need you to drink this all up now."

After only a few minutes, the black kitten seemed to be full. "I think he's dozed off again," Lily said when his mouth remained closed. She put the dropper on the table, then stood up, carrying the kitten as carefully as if he were a precious jewel.

"Can you manage?" Mum asked, watching her.

"Yes, thanks," Lily said, lowering him back into the box. She felt really proud of herself as she watched him snuggle snoozily against his brother. "Shall I feed the other one, too?"

"Please," Mum said. "Thanks, Lils, you're being really helpful. But you need to go straight up to bed afterwards, all right? Mrs Butler won't be very pleased with me if you fall asleep in school tomorrow."

"OK," Lily replied. She slid her hand under the black-and-white kitten and cupped her other hand protectively over the top of him while she lifted him up. Then she held him close to her chest as she went back to her chair and sat down.

"You're a natural," Mum told her, and Lily glowed with pride. She couldn't think of anything nicer than looking after animals. She had already decided to follow in Mum's footsteps and work for the RSPCA when she was a grown-up.

Like his brother, the black-and-white kitten was keen to drink the warm milk, and before long, Lily had to refill the dropper for more. "What a hungry boy you are," she said, watching him suck contentedly. "He's drinking lots, Mum."

"Good," said Mum. "I wish this little one would do the same. Come on, puss. You can do it." Lily could see that her dropper had plenty of milk left.

Once the black-and-white kitten was full, Lily put him back in the box. She yawned and Mum noticed at once. "Back to bed now, Lily," she told her. "You'll be too tired to help me with the kittens tomorrow if you don't have enough sleep tonight."

Lily hesitated. She didn't want to leave the kittens just yet. "Do you think she'll be all right?" she asked. "The tabby, I mean. Has she had much to drink yet?"

"A few drops," Mum replied, putting her back into the box. "It's not much, but it's something. And she's so small that even a tiny bit of milk will help. Fingers crossed anyway."

Lily crossed as many fingers as she could. "Can I do anything else to help?" she asked, still unwilling to go upstairs. "Should I wipe them for you, or. . .?"

"You've done plenty," Mum said. "I can manage the rest. Thank you." She gave Lily a hug and kissed the top of her head. "Off you go now, before those bare feet of yours turn to ice blocks."

Lily could hear the wind rattling the branches of the trees outside, and the rain was now beating against the windows. "Will the kittens be warm enough in here with just a hot-water bottle?" she asked, pausing in the doorway. "It feels quite cold tonight."

"I'll refill their hot-water bottle to keep them cosy," Mum said, "but you're right, it is chilly. I think I'll put their box down by the radiator, for some extra warmth. It's on a thermostat, so if the temperature drops too low, the radiator will come on and warm the room."

"OK," Lily said sleepily. She really was feeling very tired now. "Goodnight, Mum."

"Night, love," Mum said. "Sleep well. I'll see you in the morning."

"Goodnight, kitties," Lily added, coming back to peep into the box one last time. "Be good and drink lots of milk for Mum."

*Especially you, Tiny Tabby*, she thought to herself, heading upstairs. Lilly slid back under her duvet and shut her eyes. Just as she was falling asleep, she remembered to cross her fingers.

# 5

Lily woke again at seven o'clock. The house was quiet and she didn't have to get up for school for another half an hour. Usually she would roll over and doze for a bit longer, but this morning she suddenly remembered the kittens. Were they OK?

She got out of bed and hurried downstairs. It seemed strange now, that time in the middle of the night where she'd come down to help Mum. Had it actually happened or was it all a dream? Rubbing her eyes, she went into the kitchen.

*No, it can't have been a dream*, she thought, because she remembered Mum saying that she'd move the kittens down by the radiator to keep them warm, and their box was still there.

But then a split second later, Lily froze in horror as she took in what was happening. Meg was standing next to the box with her head inside it. What was she *doing*?

"Come away, Meg," Lily ordered, her heart pounding. She was terrified that something awful had happened. What if Meg had hurt the kittens? What if she'd *eaten* them? "Meg!" she cried again. "Come here!"

Meg looked confused at Lily's stern tone and her tail drooped. She was a gentle dog but playful, too. What if she'd thought the kittens were new toys for her — cuddly soft toys to chew and throw around?

"MUM!" Lily yelled at the top of her voice. "MUUMMMM! Come quick!"

She ran over to the box, scared of what she might find but knowing she had to stop Meg. She grabbed Meg's collar and tugged her away from the kittens.

Mum rushed in at that moment,

pulling her dressing gown around her, her hair wild from being in bed. "What's happened? What's going on?" she cried anxiously.

"Meg was. . . I don't know what she's done," Lily gabbled. "She had her head in the box and. . ." She swallowed. "I thought she was hurting the kittens."

Mum hurried over to the kitten box and crouched down next to it. "It's OK, they're fine," she said in the next breath, sounding every bit as relieved as Lily now felt. "In fact, they. . ." She frowned in surprise and crouched down for a closer look. "Their fur's damp," she said. "I think. . . I think Meg must have been licking them."

Meg made a small whining sound in her throat as if she was confused by all the shouting.

"It's all right, Meg," said Mum, reaching over to pat her. "Let her go, Lily, there's no harm done."

Lily relaxed her grip on Meg's collar and watched uncertainly as Meg trotted back to the kitten box and put her head inside. Her tail started wagging.

"What's she doing?" Lily asked, unable to see from where she was standing.

Mum beckoned her over. "Come and look," she said in a low voice, her eyes bright.

Lily went to crouch beside Mum, still feeling nervous, even though Mum was smiling. But as she neared the box, she saw that Mum was right — Meg was gently licking the kittens all over.

"Just as if she's their mother," Mum said, sounding touched. "Oh Meg," she said, giving the dog a stroke. "Aren't you

looking after them beautifully?"

"I think the kittens like it," Lily said, still watching.

"They certainly seem very calm," Mum agreed. "This is what the mother cat would have done, had she been here. I'm sure it must feel comforting to the kittens, having a larger animal look after them in this way." She patted Meg and got to her feet. "Now I'd better mix up some milk.

They'll be hungry again soon."

They heard the thump of footsteps coming down the stairs, and then Jacob and Max burst into the kitchen in their matching *Star Wars* pyjamas. "Talking of hungry. . ." Mum laughed. "Morning, boys. Looks like everyone wants their breakfast."

"Why was Lily shouting?" Jacob asked, his hair standing on end as it always did first thing in the morning.

"What's happening?" Max asked. "Has Lily done something naughty?"

Mum and Lily looked at each other and laughed. "Definitely not," Mum replied. "She and Meg have been taking care of the kittens brilliantly."

Lily helped Jacob and Max pour some cereal, then ate her own breakfast. Dad came down and made coffee for Mum and him, while Mum whisked up a new batch of the kitten milk. Meg, meanwhile, curled up next to the kitten box as if she was protecting her babies.

"I see we have a new guard dog," Dad joked. "Has she adopted the kittens as members of her pack?"

Lily told Dad what Meg had been doing, and he leaned down and ruffled Meg's coat. "I wonder if seeing you hand-rear the kittens has brought back a faint doggy memory of when you did the same for her?" he said thoughtfully to Mum.

Mum took the tabby kitten out of the box and sat down to feed her. "You never know," she said. "It might just be her own mothering instinct coming out. It's lovely to see anyway. Isn't that right, kitty?" She gently prised open the tabby's mouth with her little finger and put the end of the dropper inside. Then she carefully squeezed out a drop of warm milk.

Lily paused, her cornflakes halfway up to her mouth as she watched, hoping that the kitten would swallow the milk without a problem. To her delight, it vanished almost at once. "She drank it!" she said happily.

"She did," Mum said, stroking the tabby's stripy fur. "She seems to be getting the hang of it at last. She had a good feed earlier, too."

"So does that mean she's going to be OK?" Lily asked, crossing the fingers of her free hand again. Hope burst up inside her like a flame.

"Well. . ." Mum bent over the tabby and didn't reply immediately. "I don't know for certain yet," she said eventually.

"It's still very early days. We need to get through the next few weeks before we know anything for sure, and all three kittens will need lots of looking after."

"I'll help," Lily said quickly.

"Me too," Jacob said. "Daniel in our class had kittens and they were so cool."

Max grinned. "They were really funny!" he said. "They played football with Daniel's marbles."

"One climbed up Daniel's mum's leg!" Jacob giggled.

"And got its claws stuck in her jeans!" Max remembered. He stirred his cereal, and a hopeful look appeared on his face. "Can we *keep* these kittens?"

Dad laughed. "I was waiting for that," he said. "I'm surprised it took you guys so long to ask!"

"Can we?" Lily asked excitedly.

"No," Mum said at once. "You know we can't keep them. Our family is bonkers enough with three children and a dog to look after."

"Oh, *pleeeeease*," begged Jacob, putting his hands together as if he were praying. "Please. We could have one each!"

"Sorry," Dad said. "Come on, finish your breakfast. The kittens are staying just long enough to make sure they're healthy

and strong. Then they'll go back to the RSPCA centre to be rehomed. I'm sure Mum and the team there will find good homes for them all."

Lily knew better than to argue, even though Max and Jacob were both pointing out that *this* was a good home and would be perfect for the kittens. When her parents said "No" like that, she knew they meant it. Still, at least they'd get to have the kittens for a few more weeks. She finished her breakfast, smiling. She couldn't wait to tell her friends all about their new house guests.

# 6

All day at school Lily could think of nothing but the kittens. As soon as Mrs Butler said it was home time, she sprinted out to find Dad in their usual meeting place, outside the boys' classroom, and bombarded him with questions. "How are the kittens? Are they OK? Is the tabby drinking more milk, do you think? What did Mum say?"

Dad held up his hands in surrender. "Whoa!" he cried. "One at a time!"

"They're all right, though, aren't they?" Lily asked. "Aren't they, Dad?"

Dad hesitated, and it seemed like the longest moment Lily had ever lived through. "Well . . . let's hope so," he replied.

Lily felt cold all over. "What's happened?" she asked, her voice shaking on the words.

Dad took her hand in his. "Mum wasn't working today, so she's been able to look after the kittens at home, but she's a bit concerned about the tabby. She's still much weaker than her brothers, apparently. Mum asked Vik if he'd pop round to have a look."

Vik was one of the vets at the RSPCA centre and good friends with Mum and Dad. "What did he say? Is the tabby ill?" Lily asked, feeling sick with worry.

"He hadn't arrived by the time I left," Dad replied. "But you and I both know that Mum and the RSPCA team will do everything they can for her, don't we? So let's try to stay positive." He gave Lily a comforting squeeze. "Ahh, here come the rascals," he said in the next moment.

Jacob and Max ran out of their classroom, both shouting excitedly. "We had Light and Dark Day today!"

"We made shadows with torches!"

"It was *soooo* cool!"

"It was epic!"

"That sounds good," Dad said, still with his arm around Lily. He squeezed her again. "Come on, let's go home."

Later Lily couldn't remember anything about the walk back. She was so preoccupied with thoughts of the kittens that a circus float might have driven by with fire-eaters and a trapeze and she wouldn't have noticed a thing. What if the vet was saying right now that there was no hope for the tabby?

As soon as they had crossed the last road and were on their street, Lily ran the rest of the way home. An RSPCA van was just pulling up outside their house when she got there, and Vik emerged a moment later, dressed in his dark RSPCA uniform. "Hi," Lily said, her heart beating even faster. "Dad said you were coming to check the kittens over."

"Hello, Lily," Vik replied. He had kind brown eyes and a calmness about him. "I'm doing a late shift tonight, so I said I'd have a look at them before I start work. Let's see how they're getting on, shall we?"

They went up the front path together and knocked on the door. Dad and the boys caught up with them just as Mum opened it. She looked quite anxious but gave a small smile when she saw Lily, Max and Jacob.

"You're all here!" she said. "Had a good day, kids? Come on in, Vik."

Lily was in such a hurry to see the kittens that she almost fell into the house. "How are they?" she asked immediately. "Is the tabby all right?"

"She's. . ." Mum broke off. "Well, Vik will tell us. This way, Vik. It's the smallest one I'm a bit worried about. She's still very listless."

Lily followed Mum and Vik into the kitchen while the boys ran upstairs to get changed. Vik crouched down and examined the kittens one by one while Lily watched, feeling tense. *Please let Tiny Tabby be OK*, she thought desperately. *Please!*

Vik explained that he was listening to the kittens' hearts and lungs. He then checked their eyes and looked inside their ears, before gently opening their mouths and pressing on their gums. "This is a test to see if the kittens are dehydrated," he told Lily, noticing her watching. "The good news is that these three have nice healthy pink gums, so we can rule that out."

"Brilliant," Lily said.

Once Vik had finished examining the kittens, he nodded his head and smiled. "Well, so far, so good," he said. "Of course, it's still touch and go at this age, but I can't see any obvious signs of infection or dehydration in any of them."

"Thank goodness," Mum replied, sounding thankful.

"You mean . . . they're really OK?" Lily asked. "Even the tabby?"

"Even the tabby," Vik assured her. "She is quite small, so we need to keep a special eye on her and make sure she gets plenty of fluids, but it sounds like you and your mum are doing a great job looking after her so far."

Lily felt wobbly with relief. Mum put an arm around her and held her close. "I've got an excellent assistant in Lily here," Mum said warmly. "Thanks so much for popping in, Vik."

"No problem at all," he replied. "I'll look forward to seeing these guys again next time you're in work."

Once Vik had said his goodbyes and left, Lily washed her hands, mindful that the kittens were so tiny that any germs could cause problems. Then she crouched by their box and stroked them lovingly.

"Hello, gorgeous ones. Did you miss me? I've been thinking about you lots today. I'm glad you're OK." She had a lump in her throat all of a sudden. "Don't scare me like that again, Tiny Tabby," she whispered, gently stroking her teeny head. "I couldn't bear it if anything happened to you."

"I was thinking. . ." Lily began at teatime that evening.

"Careful," teased Dad. "Don't want that brain of yours overheating."

Lily pulled a face at him. "I was thinking we should name the kittens," she said, the words tumbling out in a rush before she could be interrupted again. There was a moment's silence after she spoke. "Because. . . I mean. . . Well, they are going to be all right now, aren't they?"

Mum and Dad exchanged a glance. "You do know we're not going to keep the kittens, don't you?" Dad said. "I just want to make that absolutely clear."

"I know," Lily replied. "But it seems silly to keep calling them 'the black one' or 'the black-and-white one' or whatever. Can't we just name them for us, while they're here?"

Mum smiled. "I don't see why not. Have you got any ideas?"

"I've been calling the tabby Tiny Tabby," Lily confessed. "Well, in my head anyway. Tiny is a really cute name for her, I think."

"That *is* sweet," Mum agreed. "How about you, boys? Got any good ideas for the other two?"

"Fang," said Max immediately.

"Stomper," suggested Jacob.

Dad laughed. "We are naming *kittens* here, not dinosaurs, guys," he reminded them. "I was thinking something more along the lines of Fluffy."

Max rolled his eyes. "No way," he said. "What about. . . Max for the black one? That's a good name."

"I think we might get a bit muddled up with two Maxes in the house," Mum said, looking as if she was trying not to laugh.

"All right, Darth for the black one then," Jacob suggested. "And the one with white feet can be Luke."

"We're not naming the kittens after *Star Wars* characters!" Lily told him. "They have to have proper kitteny names. Like . . . Sooty. Or Smudge. Or Mr Whiskers. Or Paddypaws."

"Paddy is a sweet name," Mum said.

"Cats do pad about, don't they? Let's call the black one Paddy."

"Oh yes, that's nice," Lily said. "Paddy really suits him."

"Now we just need to name the black-and-white one," Dad said. "The one who looks like he's wearing white socks."

"SOCKS!" Jacob and Max cried at the same time.

"We could call him Socks," Jacob added, just in case anyone hadn't heard them.

"Socks is a totally cool name," Max agreed.

"Paddy, Socks and Tiny," Mum said, trying the names out together. "Perfect."

*Woof*! went Meg, as if she agreed.

"Paddy, Socks, Tiny *and Meg*," Lily corrected Mum, stroking Meg with a smile. "You're a very important member of the gang, right?"

"The most important," Mum said. "Goodness, what a full house we're going to be for a while."

Lily smiled and went on eating her tea. *What a full, happy house we are*, she thought to herself. She was so glad that Paddy, Socks and Tiny had come to stay!

# 7

Every morning for the next few days, Lily sprang out of bed and hurried downstairs as soon as she woke up. Even though Tiny was feeding as well as her brothers now, she knew that if any of the kittens became too cold or picked up an infection, they would be at risk. She dreaded anything going wrong. Already the kittens felt as if they'd been part of the family for ages.

Meg clearly agreed. Mum took the kittens into work with her, but whenever they were at home, Meg took on the role of Second Mummy. She was always leaning into the box so that she could give the kittens a wash with her tongue, or comfort them if they were squeaking.

Three days after the kittens had come to stay, Lily had a big surprise when she peeped in their box. The black kitten was staring right back at her. His eyes had opened!

"He can see!" she exclaimed, crouching down and stroking the black kitten. "Hello, Paddy. I'm Lily!"

Mum was already in the kitchen, giving Meg her breakfast. She came over to look. "Oh yes!" she said. "They must have only just opened – they weren't like that when I fed him an hour ago." She reached in and gently picked up the other two to check them. "Socks and Tiny still have their eyes closed," she said. "But they should open soon. Maybe even by the time you get home from school."

"Do I have to go to school today?" Lily asked hopefully. "I want to be here when it happens."

"Nice try," Dad said. He was stirring porridge at the stove. "Yes, you jolly well do have to go to school, Lily Hart. Here, have some of this porridge, then go and put your uniform on. And where have those boys got to?"

Jacob and Max thundered downstairs a

few minutes later, and they too were very excited that the black kitten had opened his eyes. Jacob pulled his craziest face at him, while Max showed the kitten his best handstand.

"No gymnastics in the kitchen," Dad said, catching hold of Max's legs and hoisting him the right way up. "Why don't you two show that kitten how beautifully you can eat your breakfast instead?"

"Oh, but Dad. . ." Jacob said, waving to the kitten and making his ears waggle up and down.

Mum laughed. "Even though Paddy's eyes have opened, he still won't be able to see very well yet," she told the twins, ruffling Jacob's hair. "You'll just be blurry shapes in front of him."

"What a shock they'll get when their ears open, too, and they can hear you noisy lot for the first time," Dad said.

"Their *ears* will open?" Max echoed. "What do you mean?"

"Well, do you see how they're a bit crumpled and squashed-looking at the moment?" Mum said. "By next week, their ears will pop up into little points, and they'll start hearing things as well as seeing them."

"Cool," said Lily. She loved discovering

interesting facts about animals.

"While their vision is developing, we need to keep them out of bright lights," Mum went on. "You know how our pupils get bigger and smaller, depending on how light or dark it is? Well, the kittens' eyes can't do that yet."

Meg finished her breakfast at that moment and went over to the kittens' box to check on her babies. She gave them each a good lick, then settled down protectively in front of the box, as if they were her puppies rather than kittens.

Lily put her empty porridge bowl and spoon in the dishwasher and went over to make a fuss of Meg. "It's lucky they've got you, isn't it?" she said. "You're turning out to be the best kitten mummy there ever was."

★

Once the kittens had been with the
Harts a whole week, Lily started to feel
more confident about them surviving.
They were steadily gaining weight by
the day and looked bigger already. Mum
weighed them on the kitchen scales and
announced they had each put on about
forty grams, which she was very pleased
about. All their eyes were open now,
although they still didn't do very much
other than sleep huddled together and
drink their milk.

Each of the kittens had become good
at sucking, so Mum began using special
bottles to feed them rather than the milk
dropper. Lily still helped whenever she
could, and always chose to give Tiny her
bottle first because she was her favourite.

One day after school, Lily had Tiny on

her knee for a cuddle when Meg came over and pushed her head on to Lily's lap as well. "Have you come for a fuss, too?" Lily asked with a smile.

Meg wagged her tail and began gently licking Tiny. It was the sweetest thing! Then, something even lovelier happened. At first Lily thought Tiny must be shivering when she felt her tummy vibrating. She was just about to tell Mum that Tiny was cold when she realized that it wasn't a shiver. It was a purr!

"Oh, Tiny!" she cried happily. "Mum — she's purring! I can feel her purring!"

Mum came over and gently touched Tiny. "Oh yes!" she said. "A tiny little purr. She must really like Meg washing her like that — and being with you, too, of course."

Lily couldn't stop grinning. She felt

like a proud mum herself, being there for the kitten's first proper purr. "It's weird because I can't really hear it, I can just feel it," she said.

Mum nodded. "Kittens grow into their voices just like humans do," she replied. "I'm sure her purr will get louder as she grows up. I'm really glad she's feeling happy, though."

"Me too," said Lily. "We're a good team, Megster, aren't we?"

Meg gave a low woof deep in her throat as if she was agreeing. Her black fluffy tail wagged back and forth. *Yes,* her brown eyes seemed to say. *We are a good team when it comes to looking after kittens!*

By the time they were four weeks old, the kittens had grown up a lot and were starting to play together in their box, rolling around and batting their little paws at one another. One afternoon after school, Lily noticed that Paddy was trying to walk for the first time. He was still the strongest and definitely the boldest, and Lily let out a delighted gasp as she saw him staggering and swaying on his feet as he lurched across the box. He looked adorable, his eyes round and bright with determination as he took one step, then another, then another.

"Go, Paddy!" Lily laughed, kneeling down beside the box and giving him a gentle stroke. "Kitten on a mission!"

Meg came over and watched Paddy in action, then nosed Socks and Tiny, encouraging them to try as well. Tiny was staring at Paddy as if she couldn't work out how he was managing to move like that, but Socks seemed keen to copy his brother. He shakily pushed his back legs up so that his bottom was in the air.

"That's it, Socks," Lily said. "Now lift up your front end as well."

Socks tried his best, but he wasn't quite strong enough to push up from his front paws at the same time as his back ones. Seconds later, he collapsed down on the blanket as if it was all too much for him.

"Oh, Socks." Lily giggled. "It's hard work, isn't it?"

Socks didn't give up. This time he pushed up his front legs first, his whiskers quivering with excitement . . . but his back legs stayed firmly down.

"You're like a little see-saw," Lily said, gently lifting his tummy in an attempt to help him. Socks wobbled dizzily for a moment as he balanced on all fours, then took a first shaky step. "You did it!" Lily cheered, just as Socks plunged down again. "Well done. Keep trying! How about you, Tiny? Are you going to have a go as well?"

Tiny just blinked her wide blue eyes, then gave a yawn and stretched. Moments later, she had curled her tail around her and was fast asleep.

"Even *thinking* about it is tiring, right?" Lily laughed, stroking her lovingly. "Maybe tomorrow, Tiny. We don't want those boys leaving you behind, now, do we?"

# 8

Two days later, Paddy, Socks and even Tiny were all walking freely around their box, and starting to chase after one another. Mum cut open one side of the cardboard so that they could venture out and start exploring the world – or the kitchen, at least. Paddy, of course, was the first one who dared to leave the safety of the box, soon followed by Socks. Tiny stared at her brothers as they skittered across the kitchen floor, pouncing on a crumb under the table, then sniffing at one of the boys' toy cars, which the twins had been playing with earlier.

She put one small stripy paw out of the box as if testing the air, then withdrew it hurriedly and backed away, whiskers trembling.

Lily was at the table, writing out invitations to her birthday party, which was in a few weeks' time. It was going to be an ice-skating party, and Dad had drawn a picture of Lily skating with Meg, which he'd printed on to cards for her. In the picture, Meg was standing on her hind legs, her feet laced into skates, with a red bobble hat on her head, striking an elegant pose. It made Lily laugh every time she looked at it.

She put down her pen to watch Tiny. "Come on," she coaxed. "Don't you want to get out of the box, too?"

Tiny showed no signs of wanting to explore, so Lily got up from the table and tried to tempt her out by rolling a little ball nearby. Tiny watched it go past and cautiously stretched out a paw in its direction, but she didn't seem tempted enough to chase after it. "How about playing with some string?" Lily suggested next and cut a piece from the roll in the kitchen drawer. She dangled it above Tiny's head and the tabby promptly toppled over backwards on the soft blanket, trying to catch it.

Lily laughed as Tiny picked herself up and quickly washed her tail as if she'd meant to do that all along. "Look, here it is," she said, pulling the string away from Tiny and on to the kitchen floor. "Why don't you come and play?"

Tiny leaned out of the box, eyes on the string, but hesitated. Paddy and Socks, meanwhile, were tussling around Mum's feet, nearly tripping her up as she put the shopping away. "Hey! Wildcats alert," she said with a smile. Then she glanced over and saw Tiny's nervous face. "Two wildcats and a scaredy-cat," she said. "Come on, Tiny! Look how much fun the boys are having."

"Shall I just lift her out, Mum?" Lily wondered.

But before Mum could reply, the kitchen door opened and Dad came in with Meg, home from a walk. "Whoa!" Dad laughed, seeing Paddy and Socks play-fighting in the middle of the floor. "I'll have to watch where I tread now these guys are on the move."

Meg gave a gentle woof and went towards Socks and Paddy. As soon as they saw her, they stopped playing and rushed over to her, almost falling over themselves in excitement to see their "mummy".

"Those boys are certainly pleased to have you home, Meg," Mum said, chuckling as the two kittens bounced eagerly around the dog's legs.

Then came a scrambling of little claws, and Lily saw that Tiny had suddenly leaped from the cardboard box, and was now hurrying over to greet Meg as well. She looked *very* excited at her own bravery,

her tiny tail up in the air, as she went to join her brothers. "You did it, Tiny! Well done!" Lily laughed. "She wouldn't dare come out of the box for me, Dad. Just for Meg!"

Meg sat down and licked all three kittens in her motherly way, then stayed patiently in the same position while they clambered over her.

"That dog is a saint," Dad said, shaking his head and smiling. "Honestly, Meg, I don't know how you put up with it!"

But Lily thought Meg looked perfectly happy, having the kittens climbing up her back or pouncing on her tail as it twitched to and fro. And the kittens seemed delighted to be able to play with her like this, out of their box – even Tiny, now that she'd plucked up the courage.

Watching them, Lily felt a mixture of happiness and sadness. She was thrilled that the kittens were so much stronger and healthier than when they'd first arrived – and proud, too, that she'd helped to look after them. All the same, she couldn't help but feel a pang of sadness that this happy little family would have to be separated one day soon. The kittens were nearly five weeks old now and Mum said that once they were eight weeks, they would probably be ready for adoption. Lily knew already that she would miss them so much when they'd gone – and so would Meg!

Over the next few weeks, the kittens became more and more playful and fun. They loved scampering about, chasing anything in sight. Then one afternoon,

Lily came home from school feeling really upset. It was Friday afternoon, and normally she'd be feeling excited about the weekend ahead, but instead all she could think about was how Tiny, Socks and Paddy had to leave in the morning to go to the rehoming centre. The house would be so quiet without them!

"Whoever gets to look after you guys next is so lucky," Lily sighed, sitting on the kitchen floor and watching the kittens romping about as usual. Socks was playing with a marble, batting it with his paws like a football, then galloping after it. Paddy was stalking an invisible mouse, by the looks of things, creeping along with his bottom in the air, nose to the ground, ready to pounce. And Tiny was. . . Where was Tiny?

"Hey!" laughed Lily as Tiny appeared

from behind her, making a sudden dart for the marble Socks was playing with. "You monkey, come here!" She scooped her up and cuddled her, feeling Tiny's heart beating fast in her chest. "Tiny girl," she said sadly, "I wish you weren't going tomorrow."

Mum came in just then and overheard her.

"Come on, Lils," she said gently, walking over and hugging her. "It's for the best. They'll be fine."

Lily swallowed hard and nodded. It *would* be fine, she told herself. It really would!

But then why did she feel so sad?

"What lovely healthy kittens," smiled Sheena, the rehoming manager at the RSPCA centre, as she peered in at them.

It was Saturday morning, and Lily and
Mum had just arrived with Paddy, Socks
and Tiny. Sheena was tall, with freckles
all over her nose and long blonde hair in
a plait. She already knew the kittens, as
Mum had been bringing them in to work
with her over the last seven weeks. "Hello,
Paddy," she said, lifting him out of the cat
carrier to check him over.

Paddy squirmed and wriggled in Sheena's hand, his eyes wide.

"It's all right, Paddy," Lily said softly. "Don't worry, I'm here."

It had been awful that morning, putting the kittens into the cat carrier together with their favourite sleeping blanket, knowing that they wouldn't be coming back. Jacob and Max had been close to tears, not wanting to have to say goodbye. Dad was taking them to Saturday Football Club, which they loved, but they didn't look at all happy as they went off in their kit.

Meg, too, seemed to have picked up on the family's sad mood and knew something odd was happening. She tried to follow Mum and Lily out of the house when they were setting off, and Lily could hear her whining when the front door was shut.

"Try to look on the bright side," Mum said as she drove away, the cat carrier down by Lily's feet. "These kittens wouldn't be here today if it wasn't for us looking after them. And now they're ready to start a big new adventure with someone else."

"I know," Lily said. Mum was right. She was proud to have helped look after the kittens – and lucky, too, she reminded herself. Her best friends, Martha and Zoe, had been so envious when they'd heard how she and Mum had bottle-fed the tiny creatures in the early weeks. Not many people got the chance to do that!

Now that they were at the rehoming centre and talking to Sheena, Lily felt a bit better. It was clear that Sheena really loved animals, and wanted to know all about the kittens and their different personalities. More importantly, she seemed determined to find the perfect families to adopt them.

"We won't rush into anything," Sheena said. "Kittens are very popular here, so I know we'll be able to get a great match for them. We always do a home visit for anyone wanting to rehome a pet, and ask them lots of questions to make sure they can look after an animal properly."

"And if we think anyone's not up to the job," Mum added, "we won't let them have a pet. It's as simple as that."

Lily nodded. That sounded good. She tried to stay positive as Sheena checked over Tiny and then Socks.

"I guess we should say goodbye, then, Lils," Mum said when Sheena had finished.

Lily didn't trust herself to speak all of a sudden. This was the bit she'd been dreading. She'd known all along they couldn't keep the kittens, but it seemed so final, having to leave them now.

She cuddled each kitten in turn, stroking them lovingly and kissing their soft heads. She picked up Tiny last of all, not wanting to let her go. "Goodbye," she whispered, her face against Tiny's fur.

She thought for a terrible moment she might burst into tears and forced herself not to. "I really loved looking after you. I hope your new owners are nice."

Mum gave her a hug. "Come on, love," she said gently. "Let's go."

"You did a great job looking after them," Sheena said. "Thanks, guys. They'll be fine with us now."

Lily nodded, feeling a sob building in her throat. Then, with a heavy sigh, she put Tiny in the box again, blinked back her tears and walked away.

## 9

Once she was home, Lily tried to put the kittens out of her mind, but it wasn't easy. Meg seemed to miss them, too, looking everywhere for them at first, as if they might be lost in the house. The whole weekend felt very quiet and ordinary without the mischievous antics of Tiny, Paddy and Socks.

"Any news?" Lily asked Mum as soon as she came home from work on Monday. "How are the kittens?"

"They're absolutely fine," Mum replied. "And someone wants to adopt Paddy and

Socks already, so that's good, isn't it?"

"Yes," Lily managed to say after a moment. She couldn't help feeling a bit upset on behalf of her favourite kitten. "Why didn't they want Tiny as well, though?"

"They probably only wanted two kittens," Mum said. "Taking on three is quite a big commitment."

"What are they like?" Max wanted to know. "Have they got proper toys for the kittens to play with?"

"You need to tell them that Paddy liked playing with the ping-pong ball best," Jacob said. "He might be sad without a ping-pong ball."

"And Socks' favourite thing was my toy sports car," Max put in.

Lily pictured Socks chasing the car all the way across the room and tried to smile, but couldn't help a sigh at the same time. She still felt an ache inside whenever she thought about the kittens.

"They're a family with young children," Mum replied. "I'm sure they'll be lovely. Sheena's going to do the home visit in a few days."

Lily sighed again, trying her hardest to be glad for Paddy and Socks. A family with young children did sound perfect, after all. The children were sure to love the kittens and spend lots of time playing with them. And at least the two of them would get to stay together. *It's for the best*, she reminded herself, even though she wasn't sure she believed her own words.

The next day, Mum had more news. "Someone wants to adopt Tiny, apparently," she said. "Well, a couple of people actually. First an elderly lady came in and just fell in love with her. But after talking to Sheena about what sort of pet would be most suitable, they both agreed that an older cat would be better. Tiny might be a bit of a handful for her."

Lily nodded, glad that Sheena and Mum were taking such care to find Tiny the best owner. It still felt strange, though, the thought of her going to live with anyone else. "What was the second person like?" she asked.

"It was a family with two children who sounded ideal," Mum told her. "They've got a lovely big garden, and they already have a couple of rabbits, so they're used to looking after pets."

"Sounds good," Lily said, trying to be pleased for Tiny, even though deep down she envied the lucky family who were going to have her.

Mum put her arm around Lily. "You're being so grown-up about this," she said. "Well done. I know it's not easy."

"If Tiny's happy, I don't mind," Lily said, even though this wasn't completely true. She did mind – a lot! – no matter how brave she tried to be.

Dad saw the expression on her face. "How about coming for a walk with me and Meg before I start making the tea?" he said. "We can take the frisbee with us to the park and have a game."

Lily smiled. "Yes, please," she said gratefully. Moping around after Tiny wasn't going to make her feel any better, she realized – but fresh air and frisbee with Dad and Meg might help a bit.

★

Mum kept everyone up to date whenever there was news from the rehoming centre. Sheena went on the home visit to see the people who wanted to adopt Paddy and Socks, and decided that they were suitable owners and could collect their new kittens within the week. The family due to adopt Tiny had now filled in all their forms and arranged a home visit, too. It was really happening.

Thank goodness Lily's birthday came along to cheer her up. Presents and treats were the best kind of distraction! Mum and Dad gave her a new red bike, and Jacob and Max gave her one roller skate each, which they thought was very funny. Cards and gifts plopped through the letterbox from her cousins, and Lily was allowed to invite Martha and Zoe home after school for her birthday tea, before her

ice-skating party the following weekend.

When she, Martha and Zoe came home that afternoon, a delicious smell of baking wafted from the kitchen. Lily just caught a glimpse of a yummy-looking chocolate birthday cake before Dad whipped it away into a cupboard out of sight. Grandma was there as a special surprise with another present and card for Lily. "Happy birthday,

Lily-pops," she said, giving one of her big squeezy hugs.

"Thanks, Grandma," Lily said, hugging her back.

"Mum will be back from work soon," said Dad, dropping a kiss on her head. "Why don't you girls go and play while we start getting tea ready?"

Lily took her friends upstairs to show them her presents, and then they decided to play hide-and-seek around the house. "I'll be the seeker," Martha offered and put her hands over her eyes. "One, two, three. . ." she began counting.

The boys were playing, too, and everyone scattered to find the best hiding place. Jacob bolted for the hall, where there was a downstairs cupboard. He always hid there! Zoe headed for the bathroom while Max ran into the living room.

Lily, meanwhile, hurried to the kitchen and was just about to squeeze into the tall cupboard where they kept the broom and mop when she caught sight of a shiny marble down in the corner by the door. It reminded her of Tiny, and how much she'd liked playing with it.

Lily had a sudden pang of missing Tiny, and couldn't help wondering where she was, and what she might be doing now. Was she living with her new family yet, with a different house to explore? Maybe she'd already forgotten about Lily.

". . . eighteen, nineteen, TWENTY! Coming, ready or not!" she heard Martha yell just then.

"Shh!" Lily said to Dad and Grandma, who were setting out plates of food on the kitchen table. Then she quickly crammed herself into the cupboard and crouched in the darkness, listening hard to try to make out where Martha and the others were. She could hear footsteps thudding upstairs and hoped that somebody else would be found first. Then she heard another sound – the front door opening. Mum was home!

"I'm back!" Mum called. "Where's that birthday girl of mine? I hope she hasn't eaten all the cake without me."

Laughing, Lily emerged from the cupboard. "Here I am!" she cried, forgetting about hide-and-seek. Then she stopped in surprise as Mum walked into the room holding a cat carrier.

"What's in there?" Lily asked. "Have you brought another animal home to look after?"

"Why don't you open it and see?"

Mum replied, carefully setting the carrier down on the floor. Her eyes were twinkling and Lily felt her heart pound. What had Mum brought back this time?

Lily fumbled to open the fastening of the cat carrier, her fingers trembling on the catch. Meg gave a sudden woof and hurried over, her ears up and her tail wagging. She sniffed the cat carrier and barked again, her tail thumping on the ground. If ever a dog could look like she was smiling, Meg was that dog.

Lily began to feel more excited than ever. At last she pulled open the door of the carrier . . . and there was Tiny!

Lily stared in delight, hardly daring to believe her own eyes. "Tiny!" she cried, picking her up and cuddling her. "What are *you* doing here?"

"Surprise!" laughed Dad.

"Goodness me!" Grandma exclaimed.
"What a dear little kitten!"

Lily barely heard them, she was so
pleased to see Tiny again. "This is the
nicest surprise of the whole day!" she
cried as Meg licked Tiny lovingly. The
kitten immediately burst into a rumbling
purr. "But what's she doing here?" Lily
went on. "It's just . . . I thought she'd be
with her new family by now." She felt
confused. Was she missing something? "Is

everything all right?"

"Everything's fine," Dad said with a grin.

"She was *meant* to be with her new family by now," Mum explained, "but they phoned this morning, very apologetic, to say that there had been a change of plan. The mum – Mrs Cartwright – found out yesterday that her office will be relocating to a different site, about a hundred miles away, next year. They're probably going to have to move house, so it's all a bit of a shock."

"What, so they don't want Tiny any more?" Lily asked.

"It's not that they don't want her," Mum replied. "They just didn't think it was fair to adopt her while they're making such a big decision. If they do move, they'll get another kitten in their new house, apparently. So. . ."

"So . . . what's going to happen to Tiny?" Lily asked, hope swelling inside her. "Is she. . . Could we. . .?" She couldn't get the words out. Surely Mum hadn't brought the kitten here just to take her back to the rehoming centre again?

"Well," Mum said. "Dad and I have been thinking. We've all missed the kittens – not just us but Meg, too. And we were talking last night about maybe adopting a cat of our own sometime. Then when Tiny's new family pulled out today, it felt like fate. So here she is, the youngest member of the Hart family back home again. And she's here for keeps this time."

Lily couldn't speak she was so happy. Her eyes shone as she snuggled her face into Tiny's stripy fur. *Back home! Here for keeps!* Already she was thinking about all the fun things she and Tiny could do together, all the games and adventures they could have, and how much she was going to enjoy seeing her grow up. She was so glad Mum had brought her home!

Martha burst into the room just then, followed by Zoe, Jacob and Max. "FOUND YOU!" she sang, and then her hand flew up to her mouth as she saw Tiny on Lily's knee. "Ohhhh!" she squeaked. "Is that another birthday present?"

"No, she's not a present," Mum said with a smile, "but she is a much-loved member of this family – and one we simply couldn't let go. Martha and Zoe, meet Tiny."

Jacob and Max whooped with

excitement and high-fived each other,
and then everyone fussed around Tiny,
stroking and petting her. Tiny purred and
purred, clearly *very* pleased to be back.

"Welcome home, Tiny," Lily said,
tickling her under the chin. She still
couldn't quite believe she was there, and

staying for good. "You've just made today the best birthday ever!"

# Epilogue

Six weeks later, Tiny wasn't quite so tiny any more! Her legs had grown much longer, and her tail was fluffier. She and Meg were as close as ever, curling up to sleep together in the dog basket every night, with Meg still fussing over her like a mother. When Tiny wasn't snoozing, she was playful and adventurous, chasing everything and pouncing on it with her front paws. She particularly liked one of Max's old white teddies and would drag it around the house as if it were a real animal she'd caught.

One afternoon when Dad brought Lily, Max and Jacob home from school, he told them he'd been working on a new painting that day. "A very special one," he said as he opened the front door to let them all in. "See if you can spot why."

Dad had hung the new picture in the hall and they crowded round to look at it. Mum was off work that day, and stood with them, her arm around Dad. At first glance, the painting was similar to the one

that hung in the living room, with the Hart family flying off on the back of a green dragon. But as Lily looked closer, she realized that this time, Dad had drawn them perched on a big red dragon . . . with an extra passenger on its back.

"There's Tiny!" Lily laughed, spotting the little kitten who was sitting behind her in the picture. Dad had painted her with a striped paw outstretched, as if she was trying to catch Lily's dangling plait. "Oh Dad, it's great!"

Dad smiled. "Well, I couldn't have us flying away for an adventure without Tiny, now could I?" he said. "Leave her behind? No way."

Lily grinned as, right on cue, Tiny bounded out of the living room and gave a great big meow as if to say, *Nobody's leaving me behind!*

"We'd never go anywhere without you, Tiny," she promised, reaching down to pick her up. "You're one of the family now, aren't you?"

Tiny purred, clearly glad about that, and Lily cuddled her close. "If I could purr, too, I would," she told the kitten. "Because I feel very, very happy."

"That's what I like to hear," Mum said with a smile. "Now then, is anyone hungry? We've got crumpets. . ."

Jacob and Max both started cheering and jumping up and down, Meg woofed and Tiny gave a gigantic leap from Lily's arms and began wildly chasing her own tail round and round in circles. Lily just laughed again. Being part of her crazy, noisy family was brilliant fun – and now that Tiny had joined them, it was even better.

# The Real-Life Rescue

Although the characters and animals in Lily's story are fictional, they are based on a real-life rescue in which four tiny kittens were found abandoned in the rain and were brought into an RSPCA centre.

Staff at the centre leapt into action to save the week-old kittens, giving them intensive round-the-clock care with bottle feeds every three hours.

When an RSPCA Animal Care Assistant took the kittens home with her at night, her pet dog Missey decided to lend a paw, too. Missey took a real shine to the kittens. She cleaned them, gave them a good lick all over, and was like a surrogate mum to them. She didn't seem to mind that they were kittens. In fact, Missey was hand-reared herself so it was like she was repaying the favour.

Four-year-old Missey, a crossbreed, was bottle-fed by RSPCA staff when her mother rejected her as a puppy. She was taken in by her owner when she was six weeks old.

The kittens – two males and two females – were named after the *X Factor* judges: Louis, Gary, Kelly and Tulisa. They were all successfully adopted and are now healthy and happy one-year-old cats. Here are some photos of them during their early weeks:

One of the kittens is hand-fed with special kitten milk

Missey mothering the kittens

The rescued kittens in their basket

# Meet A Real RSPCA Worker
# – Kirsty Martuccio

Cattery Supervisor, RSPCA Gonsal Farm
Animal Centre

**Lily's story is based on a real–life
animal rescue. Could you tell us about
a similar rescue you were part of?**
Unfortunately, the RSPCA often deal with
abandoned kittens. I looked after three

kittens that were thought to be about one week old. They were very small, their eyes were still closed and their ears curled. Like Lily's story, one was smaller than the others, but with careful hand-rearing all three survived.

Sometimes kittens are brought in by members of the public who have heard a noise and found a bag or box with the kittens in under a bush or abandoned in a car park or rubbish bin. This might be because the mother cat hasn't been neutered and unexpectedly had kittens. The owner might be dumping the kittens rather than taking responsibility for them.

Sometimes an Inspector or Animal Collection Officer will be called to collect the kittens. Occasionally someone might leave them by the entrance to an Animal Centre and the staff will find them in the morning. The RSPCA always look after them and work to find them happy new homes.

**How do you treat newborn kittens?**
All newborn kittens, if abandoned and not
with mum, are hand-reared. They will be
allocated to a member of staff who will
take care of them twenty-four hours a day,
including taking them home after a long day
at work to give them nightly feeds. They
will be fed by a special kitten-rearing bottle
with special kitten milk and are closely
observed to ensure they are gaining weight
and feeding well. They are also toileted after
each feed, burped (like a baby) and kept
warm with blankets and heat pads.

Sometimes, if a kitten doesn't take well
to a bottle, we will try to adopt them on to
another nursing mum in the cattery. To do
this, you have to exchange scents by rubbing
the kitten on the mum and keeping a very
close eye to ensure that she accepts them.
It doesn't always work but occasionally they
are natural mummies and will just roll over
and accept them, which is lovely.

## Why did you want to work for the RSPCA?

I've always had a strong interest in feline nursing care and behaviour, and to work for the RSPCA is something I'd always dreamed of doing.

I have a huge amount of respect and passion for the work the RSPCA does, especially at the rehoming centres. Abandonment of animals is sadly increasing, making the RSPCA's job harder and harder. Saying that, it's the best job in the world being involved with rescuing animals and seeing them finally have the life they all deserve – a truly rewarding job which I wholeheartedly enjoy!

## Could you describe what a typical day at work is like?

This is tricky! Every day is different! You have the routine work, which will be feeding and cleaning the cats. Once this is completed, there will be general health checks and treatments, such as flea or worm medication. Grooming is a daily task, as well as general stimulation and socialization between cats.

Cats come in at any time, so they need health checking and assessing. We also work with the public on a daily basis, trying to find the right cat for them and their lifestyle. People think it's just a matter of coming in and picking whichever one they like, but that's not always the case due to some of the cats' histories – for example, mistreatment. Also, we try and promote animals regularly, keeping the press releases going and featuring cats that have been with us a long time, etc. No day is planned or the same – that's what keeps it so interesting and fun!

## What is the best thing about being a Cattery Supervisor?

The best thing about being a Cattery Supervisor is the freedom to do as much as I can to get these animals into the right homes! I work with such a great team of staff and have wonderful managers who aren't afraid to try new approaches to get the animals' stories out there and reach our goal – finding them their forever home!

## To find out more about the work the RSPCA do, go to:

**www.rspca.org.uk**

# Some Tips for Looking After Your Cat

- Interact with your cat. Gentle petting and handling of your kitten when they are young will help strengthen the bond between you and your new cat. Just make sure you clean your hands before and after handling them.

- Get some cat toys. Cats are playful and love to get rid of their energy by playing with toys. You can even make your own using old socks and ping-pong balls! Just make sure any toys are safe for your pet.

- Ask an adult to buy a tall, strong scratch post to help keep your cat's claws short and to avoid your furniture getting damaged.

- It is important that your cat eats a suitable, balanced diet, and always has access to clean drinking water.

- Litter trays should be cleaned at least once a day, or more often if needed.

- Your cat should have a comfortable, dry, draught-free, clean and quiet place to rest undisturbed. Safe hiding places to go to when they are feeling afraid are important too.

# Facts About Cats

- A group of cats is called a "clowder".

- Female cats tend to be right pawed, while male cats are more often left pawed.

- Cats can jump up to five times their own height and sometimes jump on to a fence, or a cupboard, as they like to be up high.

- Cats use a variety of sounds to communicate, including purrs, meows, trills, chirrups, growls, yowls and hisses.

- Cats can give birth to a litter of between one and nine kittens.

- A cat usually has about twelve whiskers on each side of its face.

- Domestic cats sleep for twelve to eighteen hours a day.

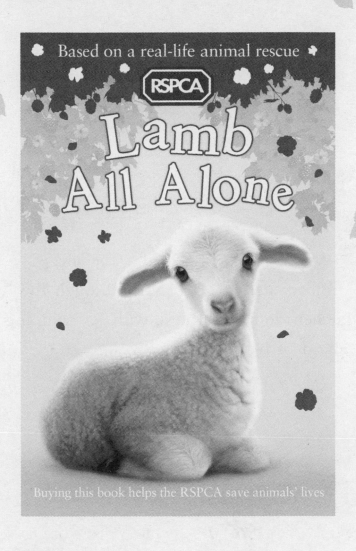

Based on a real-life animal rescue

RSPCA

Lamb
All Alone

Buying this book helps the RSPCA save animals' lives

Take a sneak peek at an extract
from another exciting story based
on a real-life animal rescue!

"Mum! Kate! The field – the sheep –
underwater. . ." Ben burst through the
kitchen door, breathless, with Jess running
ahead of him.

"Slow down," said Mum as Ben struggled to get his words out. "Start again. What's going on?"

"The bottom field has flooded! And Mr Green's sheep are still out there!"

"What? No way – he should have moved them by now," said Kate.

"Come and look!" said Ben, running back down the hall with Kate and Mum following close behind. Ben stood aside so they could peer through the steamed-up glass of the back door to see for themselves.

Kate shook her head. "Those sheep – and those lambs! They're so tiny! We've got to call Mr Green!"

"Do you have his number, Mum?" said Ben.

"Yes, it's on the fridge. . ."

Ben dashed back to the kitchen and

scanned the front of the fridge. It was covered in bills, receipts and family photos, held up by embarrassing magnets from holidays they'd been on years ago – but he couldn't see Mr Green's number anywhere.

Just as he was losing hope, he lifted up a bank statement to see if anything was underneath it. And there it was – a scrap of paper with "Mr Green" scrawled on it, peeping out from under a pineapple-shaped magnet. He snatched it up and ran back to give it to Mum.

"Brilliant, Ben," said Mum. She picked up the phone and dialled quickly. Ben and Kate watched her anxiously, waiting for Mr Green to pick up. But Mum just frowned and looked at the receiver.

"There's no dial tone," she said. "The phone lines must be down."

She grabbed her mobile from the kitchen table and dialled the number again. Ben held his breath.

"No reception!" she cried.

"Don't worry, Mum — let me try," said Kate, taking her mobile out of her pocket. "I always get reception at the bottom of the garden."

Kate grabbed the scrap of paper, pulled her soaking wet raincoat and wellies on again, and ran to the back door. Jess scampered after her, barking, thrilled at having another opportunity to chase someone.

"Hold Jess! Don't let her come after me," called Kate as she banged the back door shut and walked out into the garden, hunching against the rain.

Ben watched through the kitchen window as Kate stood by the garden fence and dialled Mr Green's number. She was getting wetter by the second. "Still ringing," she mouthed.

"Why isn't he picking up?" asked Ben. But then Kate made a thumbs-up sign, and started chatting animatedly on the phone.

"At last!" said Mum, squeezing Ben's shoulder. Ben gave a sigh of relief – but when he looked back at Kate, she seemed worried again.

"Now what?" asked Ben as Kate ran back to the house.

"It's no good – he can't come," said Kate. "He's stuck at the farm – a tree has fallen down and there's no way he can get across the road. We're going to have to think of some other way to get those sheep out of there."

No one said anything for a minute.

"Do you think *we* could get them out?" asked Ben. "I've watched Mr Green herd his sheep. . ."

"But we aren't trained herders," said Mum. "It would be dangerous to try moving them when we don't know what we're doing – we might end up scaring them into even deeper water."

They were silent again. *This is so silly*, thought Ben. *If I was stuck at the bottom of the field and couldn't get out, Mum would call an ambulance, or maybe the fire brigade. There should be something like that for animals.*

And then he realized there was. "Why don't we call the RSPCA?" said Ben.

"Of course! Yes!" said Kate. "Brilliant idea. Why didn't I think of that?"

"Because I'm cleverer than you," said Ben, making a face. Kate made one back – but then she gave him a sloppy kiss on the cheek. Ben wiped it off with his sleeve.

Mum nodded. "That's a great idea, Ben," she said. "Let's give them a call. I think they have a twenty-four-hour number for emergencies. Let's hope they're not too tied up with all the other flooding in the area."

Kate jumped up. "The internet's working on my phone – I'll get the number. Keep your fingers crossed!"

She loaded the RSPCA website on her phone and ran back to the bottom of the garden to dial the number. Ben pulled on his wellies and raincoat and followed Kate. As she waited for the RSPCA to answer, he stood on tiptoes and peered over the garden fence at the sheep in the field below. The hill where the sheep were standing was almost

covered in water now. Ben felt helpless –
he was so close to them, but there was
nothing he could do. "Please let the
RSPCA get here soon," Ben whispered
to himself. . .

*Lamb All Alone* is available
in all good bookshops.

# Collect the whole series...

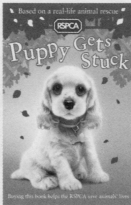

Coming in
October 2013

# Join the RSPCA!

## You'll receive:

- **six issues of *animal action* magazine**
- **a brilliant welcome pack**
- **a FAB joining gift**
- **and a FREE gift with every issue.**

Go to: **www.rspca.org.uk/ theclub**

Ask an adult to call:
**0300 123 0346** and pay by debit/credit card.

**ALL FOR £15!**
(£22 OVERSEAS)

RSPCA, Wilberforce Way, Southwater, Horsham, West Sussex RH13 9RS
The RSPCA helps animals in England and Wales. Registered charity no. 219099

DATA ON MINORS IS NEVER DISCLOSED TO THIRD PARTIES AND WE DO NOT SEND DIRECT MARKETING FUNDRAISING
LITERATURE TO UNDER 18S. PLEASE ALLOW 28 DAYS FOR DELIVERY.                                    AASCH12

**For more information on the Animal Action Club check out: www.rspca.org.uk/theden**

# You'll also love...

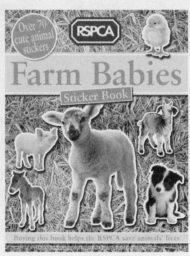

Packed with cute
stickers and fun facts!